BOB BOOKS

SET 2
Advancing Beginners

SCHOLASTIC INC.

The publisher does not have any control over and does not assume any responsibility for author or third-party websites or their content.

No part of this publication may be reproduced, stored in a retrieval system, or transmitted in any form or by any means, electronic, mechanical, photocopying, recording, or otherwise, without written permission of the publisher. For information regarding permission, write to Scholastic Inc., Attention: Permissions Department, 557 Broadway, New York, NY 10012.

Copyright © 1999 by Bobby Lynn Maslen. All rights reserved. Published by Scholastic Inc., *Publishers since 1920*. Published by arrangement with Bob Books® Publications LLC. SCHOLASTIC and associated logos are trademarks and/or registered trademarks of Scholastic Inc. BOB BOOKS are trademarks and/or registered trademarks of Bob Books® Publications LLC.

Lexile® is a registered trademark of MetaMetrics Inc.

ISBN 978-1-5461-0326-4

10 9 8 7 6 5 4 3 2 1   24 25 26 27 28

Printed in China   68

This edition first printing, February 2024

Welcome to the World of Bob Books® Advancing Beginners!

Picture your child with bright eyes, saying the magical words, "I read the whole book!"®

- The use of three-letter words and consistent short vowel and consonant sounds continues in this set, giving children words to depend on. They learn to blend more sounds into words and sentences.

- Humor and drama are emphasized in John Maslen's hilarious yet gentle illustrations.

- To increase children's comprehension and enjoyment, talk about the meaning and feelings in each story.

- Children should learn short vowel sounds such as "a," the beginning sound of apple; "e" elephant; and "i" inchworm.

- Consonant sounds, also consistent, can be taught the same way: "m" as in moon, "t" as in table.

- Words in each book are noted on the last page, organized into word families to make reading easy. Sight words become easier as beginners anticipate logical words in the story.

10 HINTS FOR TEACHING YOUR CHILD TO READ

Learning to read should be easy and fun. Here are Master Teacher Bobby Maslen's suggestions for teaching children to read:

1. Read books to your child that have stories and pictures that you enjoy. At the library, pick books that are age appropriate. Let your reader make choices.

2. In the car, point out signs that you see often. Repeat the words.

3. Play word games. Think of an animal that begins with A. Take turns, gradually advancing through the alphabet. Help when needed.

4. Keep magnetized letters on the refrigerator. Ask for the first letter in your child's name in this way: "Where is *mmm* for Mary? Here it is! Good!" If the child does not find the right letter, name the letter she found, then look for the correct letter.

5. Use alphabet blocks or tiles for forming short words. Make short sentences.

6. Use thick sidewalk chalk. Write large letters. Say the beginning sounds. Encourage the child to touch the letters and to walk on them. Make it a game.

7. Compliment drawings, writing, and reading by remarking on good work.

8. Draw road maps for playing with small cars. Arrange so the child is crossing his or her midline in the activity.

9. Present toys that develop hand-eye coordination.

10. Encourage play inside, outside, in sand, water, and on safe climbing structures, swings, and slides. All of these will develop skills that will be useful and fun in learning to love reading.

© 2006 by Lynn Maslen Kertell

Fun in the Sun

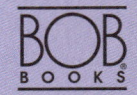

Advancing Beginners
Book 1

BOB BOOKS

Lexile® Measure: 140L
Guided Reading Level: C
Scholastic Reading Level: K
Word Count: 63

Fun in the Sun

by Bobby Lynn Maslen
pictures by John R. Maslen

Scholastic Inc.

The sun was hot.

Pop had a top hat.

Mom had a red wig.

Peg had a big cap.

Pop got the red wig.

Mom got the big cap.

Peg got the top hat.

Mom, Pop, and Peg sat in the sun.

Mom was O.K.

Peg was O.K.

Pop was hot!

Pop, Mom, and Peg had fun in the hot sun.

The End

List of 22 words in Fun in the Sun

Short Vowels

Aa	Ee	Ii	Oo	Uu	sight
and	end	big	got	fun	a
cap	Peg	in	hot	sun	O.K.
had	red	wig	Mom		the
hat			Pop		was
sat			top		

Up, Pup

Advancing Beginners
Book 2

BOB BOOKS

Lexile® Measure: BR
Guided Reading Level: E
Scholastic Reading Level: K
Word Count: 45

Up, Pup

by Bobby Lynn Maslen
pictures by John R. Maslen

Scholastic Inc.

Bet was Bob's kid.

Pug was Bet's dog.

Bud was Pug's pup.

Bob sat on a rug.

Bet sat on Bob.

Pug sat on Bet.

Bud sat on Pug.

Bob was up.

Bet was up.

Pug was up.

Bud was on top.

Uh-oh!!

The End

List of 17 words in Up, Pup

Short Vowels

Aa	Ee	Ii	Oo	Uu	sight
sat	Bet	kid	Bob	Bud	a
	end		dog	Pug	the
			on	pup	uh-oh
			top	rug	was
				up	

Pip and Pog

Advancing Beginners
Book 3

BOB BOOKS

Lexile® Measure: 100L
Guided Reading Level: D
Scholastic Reading Level: K
Word Count: 49

Pip and Pog

by Bobby Lynn Maslen
pictures by John R. Maslen

Scholastic Inc.

Pip was a pig.

Pip had a big car.

Pog was a dog.

Pog had a red car.

Pog ran into Pip.

Pip ran into Pog.

Bop!

A cop saw Pog.

A cop saw Pip.

STOP!

Pog did. Pip did.

Now Pog and Pip do not hit!

The End

List of 24 words in Pip and Pog

Short Vowels

Aa	Ee	Ii	Oo	sight
and	end	big	bop	a
had	red	did	cop	car
ran		hit	dog	do
		pig	not	into
		Pip	Pog	now
			stop	saw
				the
				was

Bow-wow!

Advancing Beginners
Book 4

BOB BOOKS

Lexile® Measure: 130L
Guided Reading Level: D
Scholastic Reading Level: K
Word Count: 51

Bow-wow!

by Bobby Lynn Maslen
pictures by John R. Maslen

Scholastic Inc.

Tip was Tim's dog.

"Yip-yap! Yip-yap!"

"Shhh! Sit, Tip."
Tip sat.

"Bow-wow! Bow-wow!"
It was Jip.

Jip was Jan's pup.

"Shhh! Sit, Jip!"
Jip sat.

Tip and Jip sat.

Tim and Jan sat.

Jip got a hug.

Tip got a pat.

"Bow-wow!"

"Yip-yap!"

The End

List of 21 words in Bow-wow!

Short Vowels

Aa	Ee	Ii	Oo	Uu	sight
and	end	it	dog	hug	a
Jan		Jip	got	pup	bow
pat		sit			the
sat		Tim			was
yap		Tip			wow
		Yip			

The Big Hat

Advancing Beginners
Book 5

BOB BOOKS

Lexile® Measure: BR
Guided Reading Level: C
Scholastic Reading Level: K
Word Count: 61

The Big Hat

by Bobby Lynn Maslen
pictures by John R. Maslen

Scholastic Inc.

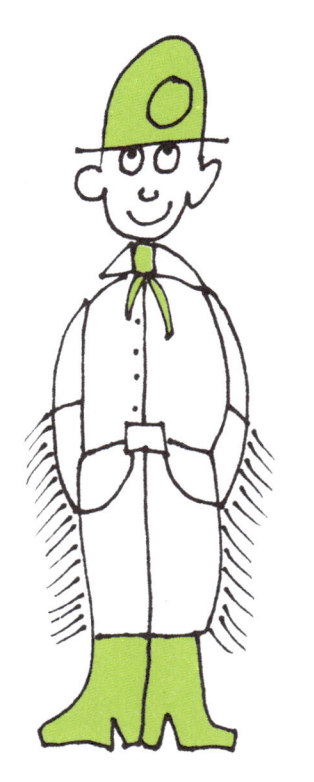

Tex was a big man.

Tex had a big hat.

Max was a cat.

Max was in the big hat.

Rex was a big dog.

Rex sat on the hat.

Rex sat on Max.

"Get off, Rex!"

Max was mad at Rex.

Tex was mad at Rex.

Rex got up.

Max was O.K.
Rex was O.K.
Tex was O.K.

The End

List of 23 words in The Big Hat

Short Vowels

Aa	Ee	Ii	Oo	Uu	sight
at	end	big	dog	up	a
cat	get	in	got		O.K.
had	Rex		off		the
hat	Tex		on		was
mad					
man					
Max					
sat					

Sox the Fox

Advancing Beginners
Book 6

BOB BOOKS

Lexile® Measure: 140L
Guided Reading Level: D
Scholastic Reading Level: K
Word Count: 71

Sox the Fox

by Bobby Lynn Maslen
pictures by John R. Maslen

Scholastic Inc.

Sox was a fox.

Sox saw a hen
Yum! Yum!

Sox hid, but the hen saw Sox.

The hen met a rat. "Run, Rat!"

The rat met a cat. "Run, Cat!"

The cat met a dog. "Run, Dog!"

The dog met a pig. "Run, Pig!"

The rat, cat, dog, and pig ran,

but the hen sat.

"Run, Hen! Run!"

The hen ran.

The fox did not get the hen.

The End

List of 23 words in Sox the Fox

Short Vowels

Aa	Ee	Ii	Oo	Uu	sight
and	end	did	dog	but	a
cat	get	hid	fox	run	saw
ran	hen	pig	not	yum	the
rat	met		Sox		was
sat					

O.K., Kids

Advancing Beginners
Book 7

BOB BOOKS

Lexile® Measure: 240L
Guided Reading Level: D
Scholastic Reading Level: K
Word Count: 76

O.K., Kids

by Bobby Lynn Maslen
pictures by John R. Maslen

Scholastic Inc.

Mom and Dad had ten kids.

Don, Dan, Jim, Tim, and Tom.
Pam, Peg, Nan, Jan, and Liz.

The ten kids sat on Mom.

The ten kids ran.

The ten kids hit.

The ten kids did a jig.

The ten kids hid in a big bag.

But the bag had a rip.

Mom and Dad saw the kids.

The kids got out of the bag.

"O.K., kids, get to bed."

"O.K., Mom. O.K., Dad."

The End

List of 39 words in O.K., Kids

Short Vowels

Aa	Ee	Ii	Oo	Uu	sight
and	bed	in	Don	but	a
bag	end	big	got		of
Dad	get	did	Mom		O.K.
Dan	Peg	hid	on		out
had	ten	hit	Tom		saw
Jan		jig			the
Nan		Jim			to
Pam		kids			
ran		Liz			
sat		rip			
		Tim			

Rub-a-Dub

Advancing Beginners
Book 8

BOB BOOKS

Lexile® Measure: 130L
Guided Reading Level: D
Scholastic Reading Level: K
Word Count: 77

Rub-a-Dub

by Bobby Lynn Maslen
pictures by John R. Maslen

Scholastic Inc.

Ann had six cats in a box.

The cats got out.

The cats got in the mud.

Ann put the cats in the tub.

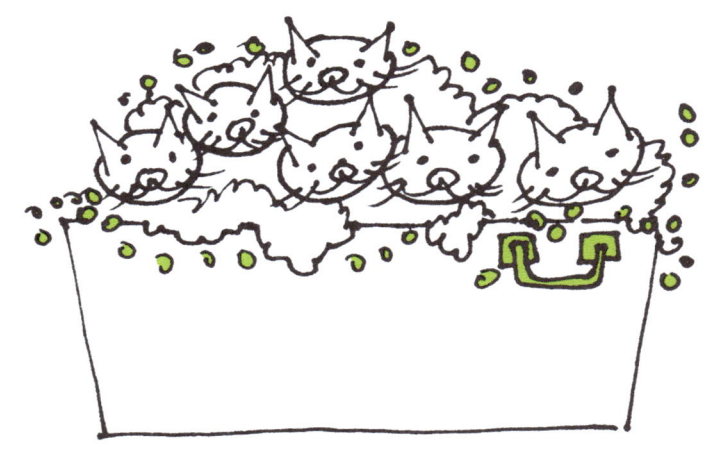

Rub-a-dub-dub.
Six cats in the tub.

Ann had to rub the mud off the cats.

The cats got mad.

The cats got out of the tub.

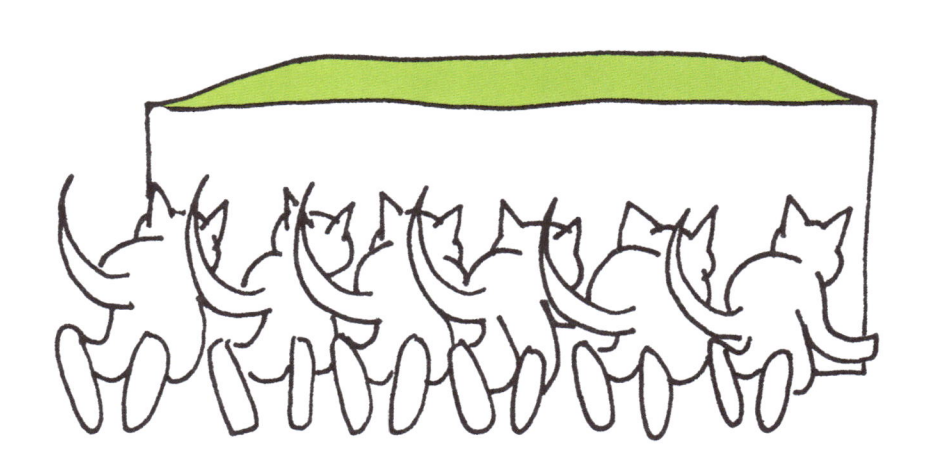

The cats ran to the box.

Ann fell.

Ann was in the mud.

Rub-a-dub-dub,
Ann is in the tub.

The End

List of 24 words in Rub-a-Dub

Short Vowels

<u>Aa</u>	<u>Ee</u>	<u>Ii</u>	<u>Oo</u>	<u>Uu</u>	<u>sight</u>
Ann	end	in	box	dub	a
cat	fell	six	got	mud	is
had			off	rub	of
mad				tub	out
ran					put
					the
					to
					was

Go, Bus

Advancing Beginners
Book 9

BOB BOOKS

Lexile® Measure: 90L
Guided Reading Level: C
Scholastic Reading Level: K
Word Count: 79

Go, Bus

by Bobby Lynn Maslen
pictures by John R. Maslen

Scholastic Inc.

Red got on the bus.

Ned got on the bus.

Red and Ned met on the bus.

GO, Bus!

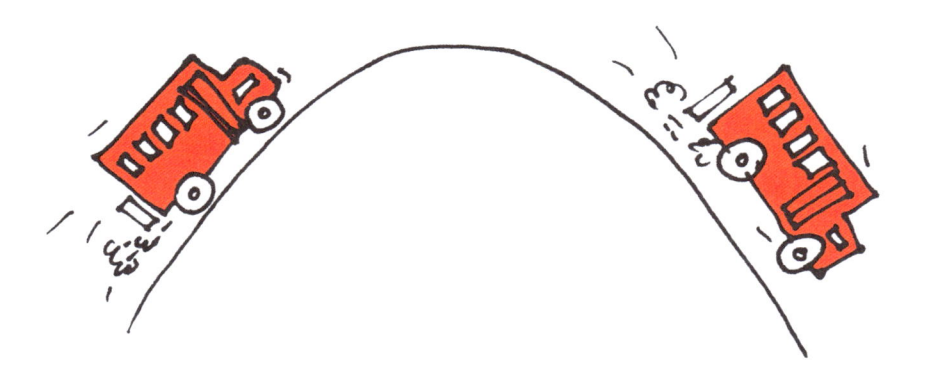

The bus ran up the hill.
The bus ran down the hill.

STOP!
The bus did not stop.

STOP THE BUS! STOP THE BUS!

The bus did stop.

Red got off the bus.
Ned got off the bus.

Dad met Red at the bus stop.

Mom met Ned at the bus stop.

"Bye-bye, Red."
"Bye-bye, Ned."

The End

List of 22 words in Go, Bus

Short Vowels

Aa	Ee	Ii	Oo	Uu	sight
and	end	did	got	bus	bye
at	met	hill	Mom	up	down
Dad	Ned		not		go
ran	Red		off		the
			on		
			stop		

The Red Hen

Advancing Beginners
Book 10

BOB BOOKS

Lexile® Measure: 50L
Guided Reading Level: C
Scholastic Reading Level: K
Word Count: 67

The Red Hen

by Bobby Lynn Maslen
pictures by John R. Maslen

Scholastic Inc.

Ben met a red hen.

The hen was wet.

The hen was sad.

The hen was not O.K.

Ben put the hen in his bed.

The hen had a nap.

The hen sat up.

"Buc-a-buc! Buc-a-buc-buc!"

The hen was O.K.

Ben put the hen out.

Then Ben saw the bed had ten eggs.

O.K. for the hen.
O.K. for Ben.

The End

List of 27 words in <u>The Red Hen</u>

Short Vowels

<u>Aa</u>	<u>Ee</u>	<u>Ii</u>	<u>Oo</u>	<u>Uu</u>	<u>sight</u>
had	bed	in	for	buc	a
nap	Ben		not	up	his
sad	eggs				O.K.
sat	end				out
	hen				put
	met				saw
	red				the
	ten				was
	then				
	wet				

The Sad Cat

Advancing Beginners
Book 11

BOB BOOKS

Lexile® Measure: 10L
Guided Reading Level: C
Scholastic Reading Level: K
Word Count: 67

The Sad Cat

by Bobby Lynn Maslen
pictures by John R. Maslen

Scholastic Inc.

A cat saw a big rat.

The rat had a top hat.

The rat had a red car.

The cat was sad.

The cat had no hat.

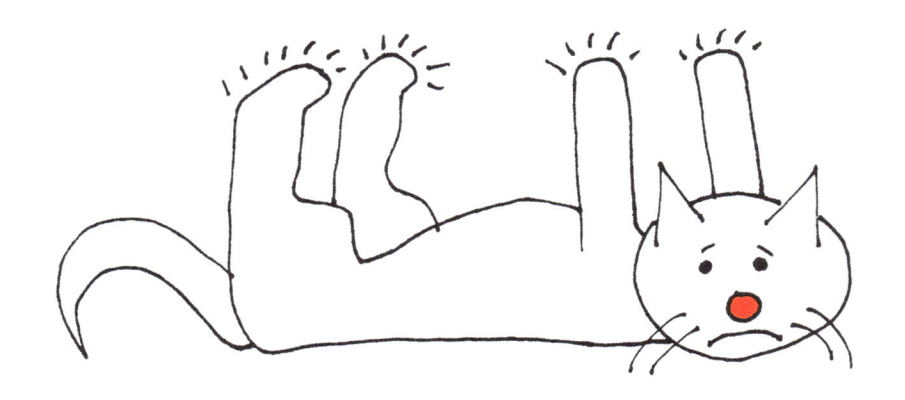

The cat had no car.

The rat had fun.

The cat did not.

The rat was sad for the cat.

"Get in the car, Cat."

The cat got in the car.

The cat and the rat had fun.

The End

List of 22 words in <u>The Sad Cat</u>

Short Vowels

<u>Aa</u>	<u>Ee</u>	<u>Ii</u>	<u>Oo</u>	<u>Uu</u>	<u>sight</u>
and	end	big	got	fun	a
cat	get	did	not		car
had	red	in	top		for
hat					no
rat					saw
sad					the
					was

0 to 10

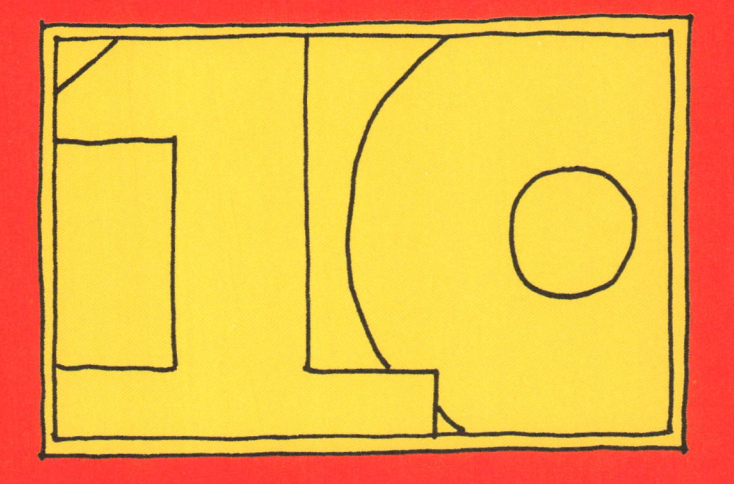

Advancing Beginners
Book 12

BOB BOOKS

Lexile® Measure: 380L
Guided Reading Level: D
Scholastic Reading Level: K
Word Count: 65

0 to 10

"Hi, pal!"

by Bobby Lynn Maslen
pictures by John R. Maslen

Scholastic Inc.

Zed had 0 (zero) beds.

Too bad, Zed.
0 beds.

Pop had 1 top hat.

Pat had 2 fat cats.

Tom met 3 big cops.

Lil had 4 lolly-pops.

Ron saw 5 wet rats.

Pam saw 6 big hats.

Peg had 7 pet hogs.

Bet met 8 bad dogs.

Sox saw 9 red hens.

Ben met 10 big men.

Ten was at......

10

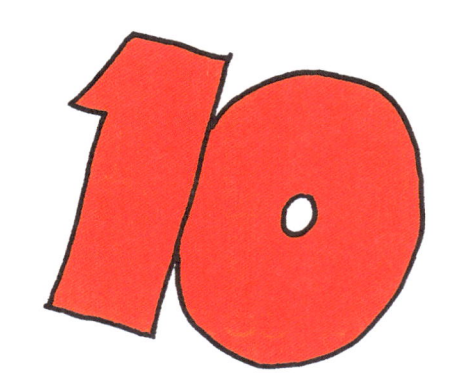

The End

List of 41 words in 0 to 10

Short Vowels

Aa	Ee	Ii	Oo	sight
at	bed	big	cop	hi
bad	Ben	Lil	dog	saw
cat	Bet		hog	the
fat	end		lolly-pop	to
had	hen		Pop	too
hat	men		Ron	was
pal	met		Sox	zero
Pam	Peg		Tom	
Pat	pet		top	
rat	red			
	ten			
	wet			
	Zed			